from the award-winning

RUBY'S STUDIO: *THE SAFETY SHOW*

A Little Book About
SAFETY

Written by: Samantha Kurtzman-Counter & Abbie Schiller
Based on a screenplay by: Ruby Vanderzee
Illustration: François Grumelin-Sohn, Laura Sicouri, Martin Carolo - *Book Design:* Rae Friis

EAN: 9780989407113--Library of Congress Control Number: 2013957739
www.TheMotherCo.com

THE MOTHER COMPANY

Hugo loves the warm sand and the salty sea air –
he's so excited and can't wait to dive into the water!

The Hippo family meets a friendly goose at the entrance. "Welcome to the Happy Herd Community Pool," she says. "Name and phone number, please."

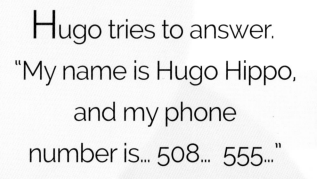

Hugo tries to answer.
"My name is Hugo Hippo,
and my phone
number is... 508... 555..."

All the numbers start mixing up in his head.
Hugo can't remember his phone number!

Mama Hippo is there to help. "It's 508-555-0873."
She gives Hugo a big hug.
"Maybe we just need to keep practicing it."

Hugo goes into the changing room,
and puts on his favorite blue swim trunks.
He's ready to swim!

"I'm heading over to the diving board, Dad," Hugo says.
"OK, I'll watch you from here," Daddy Hippo replies.

SAFETY TIP
— NO. 3 —
Make sure you can always see your Safe Adults and they can always see you!

Hugo decides today he's going on the super-sky-high diving board. He climbs the stairs all the way to the tippy-top.

But once Hugo gets to the top, he feels scared. He gets shaky and his tummy feels tingly. "Uh-oh. NO WAY. Too high," he thinks and decides to climb back down.

SAFETY TIP
— №. 4 —
It's ok to say "no" if you are scared or something feels uncomfortable. Pay attention to your "uh-oh feeling" inside and take action to keep yourself safe.

As Hugo goes down the stairs, he isn't scared anymore. He stops shaking and his tummy feels fine.

"Smart choice, dude," the toad says to Hugo. "You can try again when you're bigger," adds the cricket by his side. "Yeah," Hugo replies. He knows he made a safe decision.

As Hugo gets ready to jump off the lower diving board, two sneaky monkeys swing down and tickle him!

SAFETY TIP
— NO. 5 —

Remember, YOU are the boss of your own body, and it's ok to say "Stop!" to anyone, even a bigger kid or a grown-up. No one should touch you in any way you don't like.

"Stop that!" Hugo says. "Keep your hands to yourselves, silly monkeys." The monkeys say "sorry" and leave Hugo alone.

Hugo takes a running start, bounces on the board and flies into the water with a big SPLASH!

After a short swim, Hugo sees an ostrich next to the pool selling ice cream. "Slugpops! Bugsicles! Frog Tongue Slurpees!" calls the ostrich.

"Could you do me a favor and go get me more Bugsicles from my truck?" the ostrich says to Hugo. "I'll give you a free Slugpop if you do. It'll be our little secret."

Hugo thinks about what the ostrich asked him to do. Even though Hugo loves Slugpops, is it safe to go to the parking lot by himself?

SAFETY TIP
— NO. 6 —
Grown-ups you don't know really shouldn't ask you for help, and they shouldn't ask you to keep secrets, either.

"No!" says Hugo.
"I have to go check with my parents first."

SAFETY TIP
— NO. 7 —
Thumbs up, Hugo!
If anyone - even someone
you already know -
asks you to go anywhere
or do anything
unexpected, check with
a Safe Adult first.

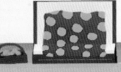

Hugo tries to find his family, but he doesn't see them anywhere! He feels scared. Where are they?

MAAAAA AAAMAAA AAAAAA!

SAFETY TIP
—NO. 8—

If you ever get lost, just stop right where you are and yell for your Safe Adult.

Hugo sees a little mouse mama having lunch with her tiny mouse babies. Maybe she can help Hugo find his family! "Excuse me, ma'am," he asks, "Can you help me find my parents?"

"Why, of course sonny!"
The mama mouse replies, taking out her tiny
phone. "Do you know their phone number?"

Hugo freezes. Can he do it? Will he remember?

Hugo concentrates really hard. "508...555..." This is the part he
always forgets - but not this time! "0-8-7-3!" Hugo smiles from
ear to ear. He finally remembered Mama Hippo's phone number!

"Hello?" Mama answers. Hugo turns his head and sees that she is right behind him. "Mama!" he says and runs into her arms.

Mama hugs her little hippo tightly. "I'm so proud of you," she says. Hugo hugs her back. "I love you, Mama," he replies.

Hugo spends the rest of the day playing by the water with his family, confident that all his smart choices will help keep him strong, happy and SAFE.

SAFETY TIP
— № 10 —
When we make smart safety choices, we can all live happy, healthy lives, together.

a note to
PARENTS & TEACHERS

Nothing is more important than keeping our children safe — but how can we talk to our kids about personal safety without scaring them? How can we be sure they know what to do to keep themselves safe when we're not around?

In **A Little Book About Safety**, we offer a modern, empowering approach to kids' personal safety. We address potentially lifesaving issues with no scare tactics and no "ick factor." Working closely with child safety expert Pattie Fitzgerald of Safely Ever After, Inc., we came up with a relatable story that kids will love to read while absorbing essential safety tools and tips they can use in their everyday lives.

When lovable Hugo Hippo navigates his way through a fun day at the community pool with his family, his safety readiness is put to the test in a variety of familiar situations. He realizes he needs to memorize his safe adult's phone number in case he gets lost, he remembers to cover up his private parts when changing to swim, he trusts his own internal "Uh-Oh Feeling" inside when deciding not to jump off the super-high diving board, and he remembers to "Check First" with a safe adult before going anywhere unexpected. These and other important safety lessons are explored gently and with humor, offering clear, safe solutions to decisions about safety that kids have to make every day.

At The Mother Company, our aim is to help parents and educators in the job of raising healthy, happy, and self-reliant children. We believe that children ought to be armed with all the information they need to make safe and smart decisions. Knowledge is power and with our Safety Series of videos, books, apps, and activity kits, we are dedicated to empowering children to be smart about safety.

For more resources to help keep kids safe, visit us at TheMotherCo.com.

— *Abbie Schiller and Sam Kurtzman-Counter, The Mother Company Mamas*

With the goal to Help Parents Raise Good People, **The Mother Company offers** award-winning children's books, videos, apps, activity kits, events, parenting resources, and more. Join us at TheMotherCo.com.

HELPING PARENTS RAISE GOOD PEOPLE WITH FUN, AWARD-WINNING BOOKS & VIDEOS

THE MOTHER COMPANY

The Feelings Series

"Edutainment at its best!"
— Daily Candy

The Safety Series

The Friendship Series

WATCH OUR TRAILERS & SEE WHAT'S NEW AT THEMOTHERCO.COM